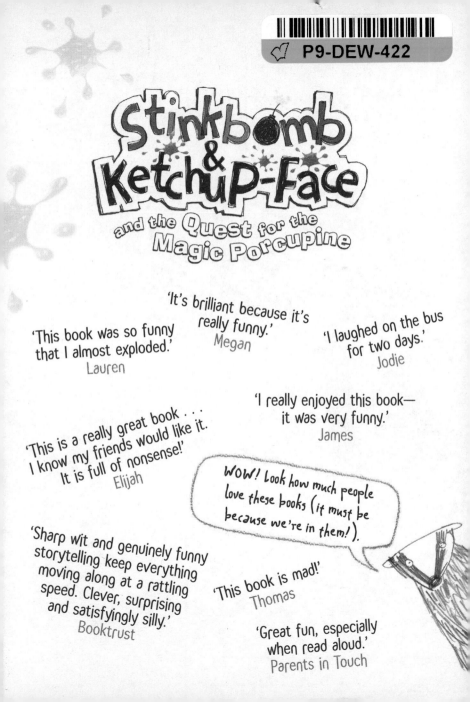

# Stinkbomb & Ketchup-Face
## and the Quest for the Magic Porcupine

'This book was so funny that I almost exploded.'
Lauren

'It's brilliant because it's really funny.'
Megan

'I laughed on the bus for two days.'
Jodie

'This is a really great book . . . I know my friends would like it. It is full of nonsense!'
Elijah

'I really enjoyed this book— it was very funny.'
James

WOW! Look how much people love these books (it must be because we're in them!).

'Sharp wit and genuinely funny storytelling keep everything moving along at a rattling speed. Clever, surprising and satisfyingly silly.'
Booktrust

'This book is mad!'
Thomas

'Great fun, especially when read aloud.'
Parents in Touch

Other books about
Stinkbomb & Ketchup-Face:

Oi! And us!

World's Best Badger

Stinkbomb & Ketchup-Face
and the Badness of Badgers

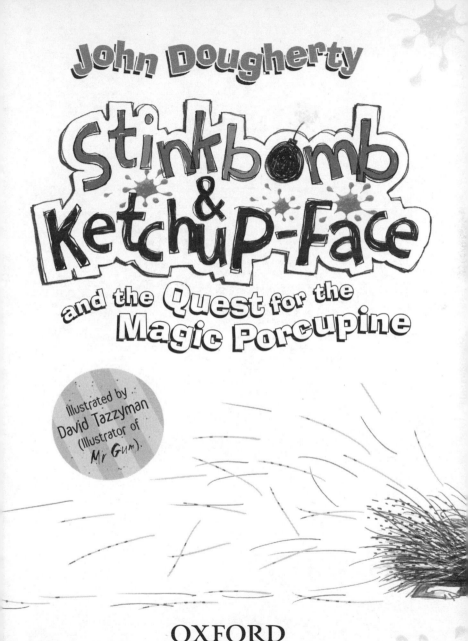

# John Dougherty

# Stinkbomb & Ketchup-Face

## and the Quest for the Magic Porcupine

Illustrated by
David Tazzyman
(Illustrator of
*Mr Gum*).

OXFORD
UNIVERSITY PRESS

# OXFORD
UNIVERSITY PRESS

Great Clarendon Street, Oxford OX2 6DP
Oxford University Press is a department of the University of Oxford.
It furthers the University's objective of excellence in research, scholarship,
and education by publishing worldwide.

Oxford is a registered trade mark of Oxford University Press
in the UK and in certain other countries

Text © John Dougherty 2014
Inside illustrations © David Tazzyman 2014
The moral rights of the author and illustrator have been asserted

Ketchup splat image by Pjorg/Shutterstock.com
Illustrative font on page 170-171 © Sudtipos

Database right Oxford University Press (maker)

First published 2014

British Library Cataloguing in Publication Data

Data available

ISBN: 978-0-19-274313-8

1 3 5 7 9 10 8 6 4 2

Printed in Great Britain
Paper used in the production of this book is a natural,
recyclable product made from wood grown in sustainable forests
The manufacturing process conforms to the environmental
regulations of the country of origin

As always, to Noah & Cara,
without whom there would be no Stinkbomb
& Ketchup-face. (There would still be badgers.
But probably not these particular badgers.) J.D.

To Kaya & Zenya,
the two stinkers next door. D.T.

Ye isle of

# Great Kerfuffle

N

W

E

S

Traffic Lights
of Waiting Rather
a Long Time

River Yuk

Old Deserted
Warehouse

Loose
Chippings

Stinkbomb &
Ketchup-Face's
house

Enchanted
Wood

**Stupidity**

Volcano
of Death

Mountains
of Doom

Swamp
of Misery

Stream

Valley of Despair

**Asillyname**

# What happened in Stinkbomb & Ketchup-Face and the Badness of Badgers,

## by Stinkbomb

My sister Ketchup-Face and I went on an adventure, armed only with our wits and a few really useful things I happened to have in my pockets.

We were brave and clever and we found the villainous badgers—who dig holes in the lawn and eat all the worms, and knock over dustbins, and frighten chickens' and drive too fast—and stopped them doing their evil and wicked doings. In the end we got them thrown in jail, and we did it all by ourselves.

Well, nearly all by ourselves. A few people helped us.

There was King Toothbrush Weasel, who's the King of Great Kerfuffle, the island where we live. And a little shopping trolley who isn't a horse, whatever my sister says. And the army of Great Kerfuffle, too, but that's not as impressive as it sounds because he's just a small cat called Malcolm the Cat.

Anyway, it was a great book.

You should read it.

What happened in
**Stinkbomb & Ketchup-Face**
*and the Badness of Badgers,*

by Ketchup-Face

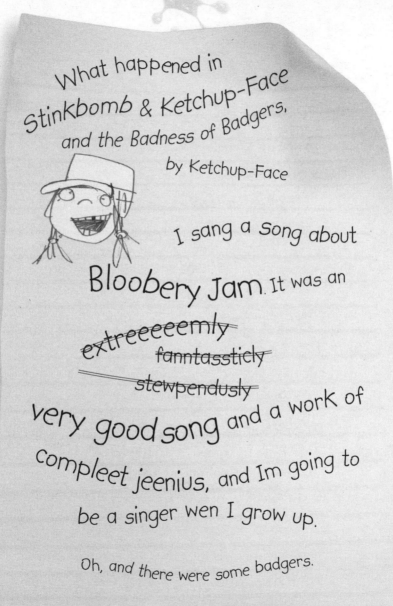

I sang a *song* about

**Bloobery Jam.** It was an

~~extreeeeemly~~

~~fanntassticly~~

~~stewpendusly~~

**very good song** and a work of

compleet jeenius, and Im going to

be a singer wen I grow up.

Oh, and there were some badgers.

What happened in Stinkbomb & Ketchup-Face and the Badness of Badgers, by King Toothbrush Weasel

Thanks to my **wise** and **benevolent** rule, peace was restored to the **Kingdom of Great Kerfuffle** and the evil and **wicked** ~~rhinoceroses~~ ~~antelopes~~ **badgers** ended up in jail where they belong.

# What happened in Stinkbomb & Ketchup-Face and the Badness of Badgers,

### by Malcolm the Cat

Actually, I'm not going to tell you.

Or perhaps I will.

No, maybe not.

On the other hand . . .

But then again . . .

It was a dark and stormy night on the island of Great Kerfuffle, and in the village of Loose Chippings the streets were deserted. Nothing could be heard but the **lashing** of the rain, and the **crashing** of the thunder, and the **thrashing** of the wind.

The rain **lashed**, and the thunder **crashed**, and the wind **thrashed**; and then they **lashed** and **crashed** and **thrashed** some more.

After a bit the rain tried **thrashing**, and the thunder tried **lashing**, and the wind had a go at **crashing**, but it sounded rubbish. So they swapped back, and the rain went on **lashing**, and the thunder went on **crashing**, and the wind went on **thrashing**.

And that was about it, really. After about half an hour, it became clear that the whole story had started too early. So it waited for a bit, and then started again.

It was a dark and stormy night on the island of Great Kerfuffle, and in the village of Loose Chippings the streets were deserted. Nothing could be heard but the **lashing** of the rain, and the **crashing** of the thunder, and the **thrashing** of the wind—until the story started and, in the village jail, something stirred.

The village jail was full of badgers. They had been there since the end of the last story, and they

3

were bored, because there was nothing to do but drive the little car **_too fast_** round the Monopoly board knocking over all the houses and hotels. They had once tried playing the game properly, but it was no fun because the smallest of them, Stewart the Badger, had eaten all the pretend money.

Now most of the badgers were staring gloomily through the prison bars at the **pouring** rain. A few were driving the little dog **_too fast_** round the board just for variety's sake, but they weren't really enjoying it, and two were sitting in a corner with the little top hat, trying to imagine it was a dustbin and taking turns to knock it over. Stewart the Badger was **snuffling** through the Monopoly box looking for something else to eat, but he found nothing except a lot of pink- and peach-coloured cards. He nibbled thoughtfully on the corner of one, pretending it was a worm, but it just didn't have the same wriggly quality that made worms so tasty. He tried another corner in case it was any different, but it wasn't.

Just as he was about to try a third corner, the card was snatched from his paw.

'What's this?' Harry the Badger asked gruffly.

'It's not a worm,' Stewart the Badger explained. 'Or a dustbin.'

'I can see that,' said Harry the Badger, turning it over and grinning a badgerish grin. 'It's even better than worms and dustbins!'

said all the other badgers, suddenly interested.

They didn't know anything *could* be better than worms and dustbins. 'What is it?'

'You'll see,' said Harry the Badger, strolling over to the door in a way that he hoped made him look cool. 'Now all we need is a handy passer-by.'

As it happened, somebody was just about to pass by the jail. His name was Blimey O'Reilly. He was out on this miserable night because he was going to visit his best friend, Gordon Bennett, and he was struggling onwards under the **lashing** of the rain, and the **crashing** of the thunder, and the **thrashing** of the wind, and the **flashing** of the **lightning**, and the **bashing** of the bats. The bats were **bashing** into him quite a lot, because their ears had got all filled up with rain and they couldn't hear where they were going.

'Oi!' said Harry the Badger. 'Let us out!'

'Please,' added Rolf the Badger, a big badger with a big badge that said (Big Badger). He didn't think being polite would make any difference, but he was anxious to make his first appearance in the story before the end of the chapter.

'Ooh, no,' said Blimey O'Reilly. 'The king said you had to stay in prison until the end of the next book.'

'I know,' said Harry the Badger. 'But that was before we found . . . this!'

He held up the card he had taken from Stewart the Badger. It said:

'GET OUT OF JAIL FREE'

Blimey O'Reilly read it carefully. 'Does it still count if the corners have been nibbled?' he asked.

'Oh, yes,' said Harry the Badger persuasively; and all the other badgers nodded and tried to look sincere.

'Oh,' said Blimey O'Reilly. 'All right, then.'

And he opened the jail door .

'Ha!' said Harry the Badger. 'Free at last!'

cried all the other badgers, and they rushed out of

the cold grey prison into the world, free badgers once more.

Then they rushed back in again. 'Yuk!' they said. 'It's raining!'

Harry the Badger rolled his eyes. 'What does a bit of rain matter,' he said, 'compared to freedom?'

'But it's *cold*,' the other badgers complained.

Harry the Badger sighed and turned to Blimey O'Reilly. 'Can we borrow your umbrella?' he asked.

'Please?' added Rolf the Badger, for much the same reason as before.

'Um, OK,' said Blimey O'Reilly, handing it over. 'But it's not very big. You won't all fit underneath it.'

'Oh, yes, we will,' said the badgers, as they scurried outside again and formed themselves into

a **tall** thin badger tower with Harry the Badger at the top holding the umbrella.

Then Blimey O'Reilly struggled wetly onwards, to a house round the corner where Gordon Bennett and his girlfriend, Maya Goodness, were waiting for him. And the tottering stack of badgers, claws glistening in the rain, wobbled off to the woods to plan some **evil** and **wicked** doings to do **evilly** and **wickedly**.

The sun had risen high, and the clouds had blown away. Birds were **chirruping** in the treetops; lambs were **frolicking** in the fields; squirrels were happily throwing nuts at one another; and a class of excited little maggots was having a party in a dead rat at the bottom of the garden.

The garden belonged to a lovely house on a hillside overlooking the little village of Loose Chippings, and inside the lovely house, in a beautiful pink bedroom, a little girl called Ketchup-Face was **snoring** like a steamroller.

In the tree outside Ketchup-Face's bedroom, a blackbird was singing. Normally, this would have been enough to wake Ketchup-Face, but on this particular morning it wasn't. So the blackbird flew away, and came back with a trumpet.

Perching on the branch nearest the window, it raised the trumpet to its beak and blew an exploratory **toot**. It peered into the wide bell.

It carefully polished the mouthpiece with one black-feathered wing. Then, like a world-famous soloist, it lifted the trumpet with a flourish, and **hurled** it as hard as it could at Ketchup-Face's head.

The trumpet bounced off Ketchup-Face's forehead with a **CLANG!!!** Ketchup-Face leapt crossly out of bed and rushed to the window.

# 'Oi! Blackbird!'

she yelled.

The blackbird blew a **raspberry**, and flew away.

Ketchup-Face shrugged, picked up the trumpet, and crossed the landing to bother her brother. But as she entered his room, she saw something that filled her with horror.

'Stinkbomb!' she cried. 'Stinkbomb! Wake up!'

Stinkbomb rolled over, grunted, and said something that sounded like, 'Hmmmph. Wombats.'

'Oh, *do* wake up, Stinkbomb!' Ketchup-Face pleaded, jumping onto his bed and hitting him repeatedly on the head with the trumpet.

Stinkbomb opened one bleary eye.

'What is it?' he grumbled.

'We've overslept!' Ketchup-Face wailed.

'What???' Stinkbomb exclaimed, sitting up. 'What time is it?'

'Look!' Ketchup-Face yelled, pointing at the clock. 'It's **almost Chapter Three**!'

And just as she spoke, the clock began to strike.

# Chapter 3

*In which the next bit of the story happens*

The clock was still bonging **Chapter Three** as Stinkbomb and Ketchup-Face shoved themselves into their clothing.

'Right!' Stinkbomb said. 'Now to get on with the story.'

'OK,' Ketchup-Face agreed. 'What are we supposed to be doing?'

Just at that moment, there was a knock on the door.

'Hurray!' said Ketchup-Face, rushing to answer it. 'It must be the story! Hello!' she added, flinging the door open. 'It's King Toothbrush Weasel!'

'I am not King Toothbrush Weasel,' said King Toothbrush Weasel. 'I am the royal trumpeter.' He pointed at his badge, which said, (Royal Trumpeter); and then he went: **'Toot toot toot tooty-toooot, toot toot toot toooooooooooooooot!'**

Stinkbomb looked at him with interest. 'Shouldn't you have a trumpet?' he said.

King Toothbrush Weasel gave him a hard stare. 'I *do* have a trumpet,' he said. 'It's probably the best trumpet in the world. It's too good to take outdoors, that's for sure.'

'Well, you ought to have a second-best one, then,' Ketchup-Face said. 'Have this.' And she gave him the one the blackbird had thrown at her.

'Oh, thank you,' said King Toothbrush Weasel.
He put it to his ear and went . . .

'**Toot toot toot tooty-tooot, toot toot toot tooooooooooooooot!**' again.

'Announcing his Royal Majesty King Toothbrush Weasel, monarch of Great Kerfuffle, ruler of the little crinkly bits round the edge, and commander in chief of Malcolm the Cat.

Toot toot toot toot toot tooooooooooooooot! toot toot tooty-tooootootoot's

Then he took off the badge that said Royal Trumpeter, and put on a small crown and a badge that said, King.

'Good morning, Stinkbomb and Ketchup-Face,' he said gravely. 'Bad news! The badgers have escaped from prison!'

'Oh,' said Stinkbomb disappointedly. 'Is this *another* story about the badgers? I wanted to be in a story about zombies this time.'

'What are zombies?' Ketchup-Face asked.

'They're sort of like crocodiles, but with two humps instead of one,' King Toothbrush Weasel said.

'Um . . . that's camels,' Stinkbomb told him.

'Nonsense!' said King Toothbrush Weasel. 'Camels are nothing like zombies. Zombies can't fly. And they don't hang upside-down in dark caves.'

'But that's bats,' Stinkbomb said.

'Bats,' said King Toothbrush Weasel firmly, 'are what you hit golf balls with when you're playing tennis. But that's not important. What's important is that we've got to catch the badgers and put them back in prison before they do any **evil** and **wicked** doings.'

'How?' Ketchup-Face asked.

King Toothbrush Weasel's face fell. 'I thought *you'd* know,' he said. 'Bother.' He took off his crown and scratched his head. Then he scratched Stinkbomb's and Ketchup-Face's heads, and then he tugged thoughtfully at his long golden beard until it came off in his hand. 'Wait a minute!' he yelped suddenly. 'I've got it!'

'No, you've dropped it,' said Ketchup-Face, picking up the beard and helping him put it back on.

'No, not the beard,' said King Toothbrush Weasel. 'I mean I've got an idea. We *are* in a story, aren't we?'

'Yes,' said Stinkbomb. 'Most of the way through **Chapter Three**.'

'Right,' said King Toothbrush Weasel. 'So to find the badgers, we need someone who knows about stories!'

'Of course!' said Stinkbomb and Ketchup-Face together.

'Yes!' said King Toothbrush Weasel dramatically. 'So, we need to go to . . . the post office!'

'Oh,' said Stinkbomb. 'I thought you were going to say "the library".'

# chapter 4

In which our heroes don't go to the post office

Just then, it began to rain.

It was not an ordinary rain. It was a horrible, inky-splattery, thick wet rain that left dark splodges on the ground and **smelt** faintly of bananas.

'What's happening?' said King Toothbrush Weasel.

'I bet it's got something to do with those badgers!' said Ketchup-Face.

'Why?' asked Stinkbomb, putting up an umbrella he had just found in his pocket.

'Because,' explained Ketchup-Face patiently, 'they're the bad guys.'

'That settles it!' said King Toothbrush Weasel. 'To the royal carriage—quickly!'

Outside the gate, waiting patiently, was a little shopping trolley with a sticker saying

stuck to its handle, and a small grey cat wearing a red soldier's jacket and a bored expression.

'Starlight!' said Ketchup-Face delightedly; for this was none other than the little shopping trolley who wasn't actually called Starlight at all, who had helped them in their last adventure.

'And Malcolm the Cat!' she added; for the cat was none other than Malcolm the Cat, who was a small cat called Malcolm the Cat, but who was also the entire army of the little kingdom of Great Kerfuffle.

'Hello,' said the little shopping trolley shyly, as they got in. 'Where to, your Majesty?'

'To the

post office!"

commanded King Toothbrush Weasel.

'Certainly,' said the little shopping trolley. 'Um . . . why are we going to the post office?'

'Because,' said King Toothbrush Weasel impatiently, 'we need someone who knows about stories, and that means a butcher, and where would we find a butcher but in a post office?'

'Ah,' said the little shopping trolley wisely, setting off at a **squeaky-wheeled gallop**, and before the sentence had finished they were pulling up outside the Loose Chippings Library.

'Here we are,' said King Toothbrush Weasel. 'The post office! Filled from end to end with all manner of books, and run by the person who knows more about stories than anyone else—the butcher!'

'But it's the—OW!' said Ketchup-Face, as Stinkbomb jabbed her sharply in the ribs. 'What did you do that for? I was only going to say that it's the—OW! Stop it! Why don't you want me to say that it's the—OW!'

'Shhh!' explained Stinkbomb.

'It's not the OW,' King Toothbrush Weasel said sternly. 'It's the post office. And this is where we'll find out how to stop the badgers doing their **evil** and **wicked** doings.'

'But it's the—OW!' yelped Ketchup-Face crossly.

'It doesn't matter what we call it,' Stinkbomb **hissed**, rubbing his elbow. 'Let's just go in and find the librarian.'

'All right,' muttered Ketchup-Face. 'But it *is* the —OW!'

The Loose Chippings Library was the grandest building in Great Kerfuffle—much grander than the Royal Palace, which was really just a small cottage with a couple of thatched turrets stuck on and a cat in a soldier's jacket standing guard outside. This was because the only sensible king that Great Kerfuffle had ever had—who was called King Sensible—had realized that libraries are much more important than palaces.

So King Sensible had ordered every spare penny in the kingdom to be spent on building a wonderful library. A hundred years later, the only

sensible queen that Great Kerfuffle had ever had—
who was called Queen Fairly Daft, because her
parents considered Queen Sensible a silly name—
had ordered it to be filled with books. This came as
a great relief to the librarians, who had been sitting
around for a hundred years waiting for something
to do.

Now Stinkbomb and Ketchup-Face and King
Toothbrush Weasel and Malcolm the Cat were
gazing up at this majestic building, hearts filled
with awe, as the sinister banana-scented rain
**splottered** and **spattered** around them.

# chapter 5

## In which our heroes enter the library, and meet Miss Butterworth

Their feet went **click**, **click**, **click** on the marbled flooring as they entered the library.

At least, King Toothbrush Weasel's did. Ketchup-Face's went **tic**, **tic**, **tic** because she was lighter and wasn't wearing impressive and kingly shoes; and Stinkbomb's went **boing**, **boing**, **boing** because he was wearing his favourite boots with the bouncy soles, and Malcolm the Cat's went , ,  because he was a cat.

Inside, the library was like a vast and silent cathedral of knowledge, except for the children's section which was full of toddlers and their mums who had come for

**Bouncy Sing & Clap Story Time with Miss Tibbles,**

and which was more like a brightly-coloured and noisy cathedral of dribbly fun.

'I wonder where the librarian is?' whispered Stinkbomb.

'*I am here,*' murmured a voice like the tinkling of wind-chimes, and suddenly, magically, the librarian appeared among them.

'OW!' said Malcolm the Cat.

'*Oh, sorry,*' said the librarian, looking down and taking her foot off Malcolm the Cat's tail.

The librarian was **tall** and thin, and dressed in black clothing of fine silk. From a sash around her waist hung a long sword. A black hood and scarf covered her head so that nothing could be seen of her face except for a pair of very sensible glasses, behind which **twinkled** wise, kind eyes. She put her hands together and bowed her head in greeting.

'*I,*' she said, '*am Miss Butterworth of the Ancient Order of Ninja Librarians. Greetings to you, Stinkbomb, Ketchup-Face, King Toothbrush Weasel, and Malcolm the Cat.*'

Stinkbomb was most impressed. 'How do you know who we are?' he asked.

Miss Butterworth bowed again. '*I am a librarian,*' she said. '*We are keepers of all knowledge. We are guardians of all books and stories. Plus, we read a lot in our lunch hour. I enjoyed your first book very much. How may I help you?*'

35

'We want to know
how to find the
badgers,'

Stinkbomb told her.

'They're making it rain a **big blobby splatty rain**,' Ketchup-Face explained.

'Which **smells** faintly of bananas,' Stink-bomb added.

'Yes!' said Ketchup-Face. 'If we don't catch them soon, all Great Kerfuffle will **smell** faintly of bananas, and it'll get invaded by monkeys and gorillas and elephants and hammerhead sharks.'

'Hammerhead sharks don't like bananas,' Stinkbomb pointed out.

'They would if they tried them,' Ketchup-Face said. 'If their mummies said, "eat up all your bananas or you won't get any sailors", then they'd try them, and then they'd like them, and then they'd invade Great Kerfuffle.'

'They don't eat sailors, either,' said Stinkbomb, who was very interested in interesting things like facts. 'They're bottom feeders.'

'Ewww,' said Ketchup-Face, who didn't know what a bottom feeder was, but could think of one or two horrid things it might be. 'So would their mummies say "eat up all your bananas or you won't get any bottoms"?'

'No,' Stinkbomb explained, 'it means they eat whatever they find lying on the bottom of the sea.'

'Oh,' said Ketchup-Face. 'So if a sailor and a banana fell out of a boat, which would they eat first?'

'I don't know what hammerhead sharks have to do with anything!' interrupted King Toothbrush

Weasel. 'Nasty little creatures with too many legs. The point is, what are we going to do about the badgers?'

*'Well,'* said Miss Butterworth slowly, *'there is one book which might help. To fetch it will be dangerous —but perhaps it is our only hope. And somebody did knock over the library bin last night, and it took me ages to clear up the mess.'* She took a deep breath, as if summoning her courage in preparation for some great ordeal—and then she wasn't there.

'Where did she go?' asked King Toothbrush Weasel.

'There she is!' cried Stinkbomb. Far above them, Miss Butterworth was scaling the **tall** bookcases towards a high shelf marked *451: Forbidden Books.*

Nimbly she climbed, dodging the traps that some ancient and long-forgotten librarian had left: a great stone ball on a chain that smashed into the bookshelf just where she had been a moment before; poisoned darts that buried themselves in the wall with a cascade of angry **phuts**; boiling lava that erupted in deadly fountains from a copy of *Top Traps to Keep Your Forbidden Books Safe*; and tribes of angry mice that appeared from behind a large encyclopaedia and poked her with tiny pitchforks.

Then she was at the top of the highest bookcase, pulling a book from the very end of the topmost shelf. As she did so, the whole bookcase shook violently. Stinkbomb and Ketchup-Face gasped as Miss Butterworth was thrown backwards into empty space, twenty metres or more above the ground.

# chapter 6

*In which Miss Butterworth is perfectly all right, and there is nothing to worry about. Except for the badgers, of course*

'Oh, dear!' said King Toothbrush Weasel, but even as he spoke the Ninja Librarian skilfully turned her fall into a somersault. Like a gymnast she twisted through the air to rebound off a large copy of *The Boingiest Trampoline in the World*. Down she came, leaping gracefully from shelf to shelf, until she alighted on the ground next to them with barely a sound.

'OW,' said Malcolm the Cat.

'Oh, sorry,' said Miss Butterworth, looking down and taking her foot off Malcolm the Cat's tail. Then she held up the book she was clutching. It was called **Stinkbomb & Ketchup-Face and the Quest for the Magic Porcupine**.

Stinkbomb gasped. 'Is that the story we're in now?' he asked, reaching for it.

Miss Butterworth snatched it away. '*You must not!*' she said seriously. '*No one without the training of a Ninja Librarian should try to read a story while they are in it. Otherwise great calamity will befall, endangering the very fabric of time and space!*'

Stinkbomb thought about this. The idea of great calamity befalling and endangering the very fabric of time and space certainly sounded interesting, but on balance he wasn't sure if he fancied it. So he stuck his hand back in his pocket.

Ketchup-Face, meanwhile, was staring up at Miss Butterworth in **awe**. She thought that the fetching of the book was the most magnificent thing she had ever seen, and she was suddenly filled with hero-worship. 'I've written a song about libraries,' she announced. 'Would you like to hear it?'

*'Yes, please,'* said Miss Butterworth.

'Oh,' said Ketchup-Face, suddenly realizing that she hadn't written a song about libraries after all. However, she wasn't going to tell Miss

Butterworth that, because it would be embarrassing. Instead, she took a deep breath, opened her mouth, and waited to see what came out.

What came out was:

'I like librar*ies*

More than climbing *trees*

More than bits of *cheese*

More than the nice lady in the sweet shop who's got hairy *knees*

And if *you* ask me *please*

Whether *I'd* like to go and sit in the *freeze-*

. . . er

I'll say: No, 'cos I want to go to the library instead because it's not as cold as the freezer and it's got lots of interesting books and stuff like that and you can use the internet and all the librarians are really nice especially Miss Butterworth and it's all lovely and anyone can borrow the books and take them home and read them · · ·

'That's a song about libraries,' she added.

*'Well done,'* said Miss Butterworth politely, and Stinkbomb gave her a brotherly pat on the back. *'Now,'* Miss Butterworth continued, *'stand back. Be still and quiet. What I am about to do is extremely dangerous.'* Very carefully, she opened the book.

Immediately, a strange **humming** filled the air.

*'Excuse me,'* said Miss Butterworth sternly, looking at King Toothbrush Weasel.

King Toothbrush Weasel blushed, and stopped **humming**. 'Sorry,' he said.

Miss Butterworth returned her attention to the book.

'Does it tell us how to catch the badgers?' Stinkbomb asked.

Miss Butterworth nodded. *'But I cannot tell you yet.'*

'Why not?' Ketchup-Face asked.

*'Because first you must say, "Why not?"'*

'I just did,' Ketchup-Face pointed out.

*'Yes,'* Miss Butterworth agreed, *'but until you say it again, I cannot tell you how to catch the badgers.'*

'Why not?' Ketchup-Face asked.

*'Because it is written,'* Miss Butterworth said, *'and all must happen as it is written.'*

'But now she *has* said it again,' Stinkbomb said. 'So can you tell us how to catch the badgers?'

*'Not yet,'* said Miss Butterworth. *'More must first come to pass.'*

'Oh,' said Stinkbomb. 'Well . . . what else has got to happen?'

Miss Butterworth returned her eyes to the book. *'Many things will happen before the secret is revealed,'* she said. *'King Toothbrush Weasel will say, "Eh?*

*What?"; a mysterious stranger in a raincoat will enter the library; the* **Number 94 bus** *will go past outside; the* **chapter** *will end, and a new one must begin; Malcolm the Cat will say,* **"OW,"**; *and then, on* **page 55**, *I may at last tell you what you must do.'*

'Right,' said Stinkbomb. 'Well, we'd better get on with it. Come on, your Majesty.'

'Eh? What?' said King Toothbrush Weasel, who hadn't been paying attention.

Just then, a mysterious stranger in a raincoat entered the library. He crossed the room and took a book from one of the shelves. Then there was silence, except for the rumble of the **Number 94 bus** going past outside.

'It's all going very well, isn't it?' said Ketch-up-Face happily. 'What's the next thing?'

'Next,' Stinkbomb reminded her, 'it's the end of the **chapter**.'

# chapter 7

In which we find page 55, and our heroes learn what they must do

'Oh, yes,' said Ketchup-Face. 'So it is. And the beginning of the next one.'

'What was the next thing, again?' Stinkbomb asked.

'*Let me see,*' said Miss Butterworth, opening the book again and taking a step towards him.

'OW,' said Malcolm the Cat.

'*Oh, sorry,*' said Miss Butterworth,

looking down and taking her foot off Malcolm the Cat's tail.

'Yes, that was it,' said Stinkbomb.

'And then we can get to **page 55** and you can tell us the secret,' said Ketchup-Face.

'But we're only on **page 50**,' Stinkbomb pointed out.

'So we are,' Ketchup-Face said. 'We'll just have to wait for a bit.'

So they waited for a bit.

'That's no good,' Stinkbomb said eventually. 'It's hardly got us any closer to **page 55** at all. I suppose we'll have to do something.'

'I could sing my song again,' Ketchup-Face suggested.

'Yes, all right,' agreed Stinkbomb.

So Ketchup-Face sang her song again.

'Bother,' said Stinkbomb, when she had finished. 'That didn't get us much further either.'

'I know!' said Ketchup-Face.

'I could shout something

REALLY REALLY LOUDLY!'

'GOOD
IDEA!'

yelled Stinkbomb, even more loudly.

*'Shhh!'* said Miss Butterworth.

'But it's working!' protested Ketchup-Face.

*'Perhaps,'* Miss Butterworth said, *'but as a Ninja Librarian, I have made vows to preserve*

the silence and dignity of the library, with exceptions only to be made for Bouncy Sing & Clap Story Time with Miss Tibbles.'

'Oh,' said Stinkbomb. 'What would happen if I just went on shouting anyway?'

'Then,' Miss Butterworth said sadly, 'I would have to chop your head off with my big sword.'

Stinkbomb thought about this. The idea of having his head chopped off with Miss Butter-worth's big sword certainly sounded interesting, but on balance he wasn't sure if he fancied it. So he decided to be quieter.

'Well,' he said softly, 'what are we going to do to get us to **page 55**, then?'

'I know!' said Ketchup-Face. 'We could ask that nice Mr Tazzyman to draw us a great big picture of a duck-billed platypus.'

'That wasn't a duck-billed platypus!' Ketchup-Face said indignantly. 'That was a hippotatomouse!'

'It looked like a duck-billed platypus to me,' said King Toothbrush Weasel.

'Never mind that!' said Stinkbomb excitedly. 'Look! It's **page 55**! Now Miss Butterworth can tell us how to catch the badgers!'

Miss Butterworth checked the page number, bowed her head in silent agreement, and opened the library's copy of **Stinkbomb & Ketchup-Face and the Quest for the Magic Porcupine** at **page 55**.

'*To catch the badgers,*' she told them, '*you must first fulfil a quest.*'

# chapter 8

In which our heroes learn of their quest

'Let me guess,' said Stinkbomb. 'Is it a quest for a Magic Porcupine?'

'*It is,*' Miss Butterworth agreed, looking up from the copy of **Stinkbomb & Ketchup-Face and the Quest for the Magic Porcupine**.

'I say!' said King Toothbrush Weasel. 'However did you know that?'

'*To stop the badgers from doing their evil and*

*wicked* doings,' Miss Butterworth continued, '*you must find the legendary Magic Porcupine of Stupidity.*'

'Stupidity?' asked Ketchup-Face.

'*Yes, Stupidity,*' said Miss Butterworth. '*It's a tiny village where the Magic Porcupine lives.*'

'Oh,' said Ketchup-Face. 'That's a silly name.'

'No, it isn't,' said King Toothbrush Weasel, 'Asillyname is in the other direction.'

'Never mind that,' said Stinkbomb, who was eager to get on with the story. 'How do we get to Stupidity?'

Miss Butterworth thought for a moment; and then she wasn't there any more.

'How *does* she do that?' asked King Toothbrush Weasel, looking round.

A moment later, just as mysteriously and silently, she had returned with another book.

'Ha!' said Malcolm the Cat smugly, twitching his tail out of the way.

King Toothbrush Weasel, curious about the book, edged closer to Miss Butterworth.

'OW!' said Malcolm the Cat.

'Oh, sorry,' said King Toothbrush Weasel, looking down and taking his foot off Malcolm the Cat's tail.

Miss Butterworth held up the book. It was called *Great Destinations for Holidays, Weekend Breaks, and Perilous Quests in Great Kerfuffle*. Turning to the *Perilous Quests* section, she found the entry on Stupidity.

*'The road to Stupidity is a long and hard one,'* she read. *'You must first cross the Valley of Despair —a terrible, desolate place filled with deadly snakes*

*—and then climb the treacherous Mountains of Doom. That done, you must make your way across the dreadful Swamp of Misery, where so many brave adventurers have perished, and if you survive thus far, you must finally face the fiery Volcano of Death, which is also a bit nasty.'*

Stinkbomb thought about this. The idea of crossing the Valley of Despair, climbing the Mountains of Doom, making his way across the Swamp of Misery, and facing the Volcano of Death certainly sounded interesting, but on balance he wasn't sure if he fancied it.

'Do we *have* to do all that?' he asked.

*'Well,'* Miss Butterworth said, *' you could take the **Number 36 bus** instead. It goes the other way, so you wouldn't have to cross the Valley of Despair, climb the Mountains of Doom, make your way across the Swamp of Misery, and face the Volcano of Death,*

although you would have to endure the *Traffic Lights of Waiting Rather a Long Time.'*

'Um . . . I think we'll take the bus,' Stinkbomb said, and Ketchup-Face agreed. 'Could we have some money for the tickets?' he asked King Tooth-brush Weasel.

None of them noticed that, while this conversation was going on, the mysterious stranger in a raincoat had crept closer to them. He was a big mysterious stranger in a raincoat with a big badge that said

As soon as he heard the bit about taking the **Number 36 bus** he turned and hurried out of the library, going as quietly as he could so as not to draw attention to himself, and pausing only to knock over the waste paper bin.

# chapter 9

In which we visit the library roof, and the cause of the mysterious rain is revealed

Outside, the mysterious stranger in a raincoat hurried up the fire escape to the library roof, where he found Harry the Badger and all the other badgers refilling their giant pump-action water guns from a big barrel of extremely dirty river water.

'Hullo, Rolf the Badger,' said Harry the Badger, pumping his water gun really hard and then **squirting** happily away. All the other badgers **squirted**, too, covering the village in a horrible, inky-splattery, thick wet rain that left dark splodges on the ground and **smelt** faintly of bananas.

The mysterious stranger in a raincoat took off his raincoat and was indeed Rolf the Badger. 'Hullo, Harry the Badger,' he said. 'What're you doing that for?'

'It's an **evil** and **wicked** doing,' Harry the Badger explained.

'Oh, OK,' said Rolf the Badger. 'Can I have a go with your water gun?'

Harry the Badger thought about this for a moment. 'Nope,' he said, **squirting** some more. 'What'd you find out?'

'Well,' said Rolf the Badger, 'apparently there's this Magic Porcupine in Stupidity that can stop badgers.'

growled Harry the Badger.

'And those kids are going to go on the **Number 36 bus** and find it.'

'Grrrrrrr!'

growled Harry the Badger.

'Then they're going to bring it back.'

'Grrrrrrrrrrrr!'

growled Harry the Badger.

'And then it'll stop us doing our **evil** and **wicked** doings.'

'Oink!'

growled Harry the Badger.

'Sorry, I mean:

Grrrrrrrrrrrr-rrrrrrrrrrrr-rrrrrr!'

'Now can I have a go with your water gun?'

'No!' said Harry the Badger, putting it down. 'We've got to stop those kids from bringing the Magic Porcupine back to Loose Chippings. How did you say they were getting there?'

'On the **Number 36 bus**,' said Rolf the Badger, still eyeing Harry the Badger's water gun enviously.

'Aha!' Harry the Badger said, looking at his watch, and then remembering that he was a badger and didn't have one. 'What time is it?'

Rolf the Badger **sniffed** the air and looked at the sky. Animals have senses that we humans don't have, and can find out lots of things by **sniffing** the air and looking at the sky. After a moment, he sniffed again, and said, 'Gosh! Did you know that Caracas is the capital of Venezuela?'

'Oooh, is it?'

said the other badgers, and they all began **sniffing** the air and looking at the sky.

'Never mind that!' Harry the Badger snarled. 'What *time* is it?'

For a moment there was no sound but the sound of **sniffing** badgers. And then one of them said, 'Um . . . . it's about five to **Chapter Ten**.'

'Perfect!' said Harry the Badger. 'The **Number 36 bus** doesn't leave till **Chapter Eleven**. We've just got time! Come on!'

'Hang on a minute,' said Rolf the Badger. 'I've just realized what that big barrel of river water reminds me of.' And he knocked it over. They watched as its filthy contents poured out and into the street below.

'Here!' said Harry the Badger. 'Who put those banana skins in there?'

# chapter 10

In which our heroes say goodbye
to their friends

A minute or two later, and an entire library nearer the ground, Stinkbomb and Ketchup-Face stood in the village square saying goodbye to their friends. Or, rather, Ketchup-Face was saying goodbye. Stinkbomb had already said it, like this:

'Bye, then.'

Ketchup-Face, however, had a strong sense of the dramatic, and felt that *Bye, then* didn't quite cover it when you are off on a quest to save the entire kingdom from **evil** and **wickedness**.

'Goodbye, Starlight, my noble steed!' she said to the little shopping trolley, trying to throw her arms around it and then giving it a kiss instead.

The little shopping trolley blushed. 'Good luck,' it said shyly.

'And goodbye, Miss Butterworth, protector of the library!' she continued, throwing her arms affectionately around the Ninja Librarian.

Miss Butterworth bowed solemnly. *'Be noble, and strong,'* she said, *'and you will succeed in your quest. Take this with you.'* She pressed something into Ketchup-Face's hand. *'Use it wisely.'*

'Thank you!' Ketchup-Face gasped, looking at the small flat object. 'Is it a magic talisman to ward off **evil** and **wickedness**?'

*'No,'* said Miss Butterworth. *'It is a library card. The mobile library stops in Stupidity most days, and I thought you might like something to read on your way back.'*

'Oh,' said Ketchup-Face. 'Thank you.' She threw her arms around Malcolm the Cat, gave him a kiss on the nose, and said, 'Goodbye, sweet little cat.'

Malcolm the Cat stared unblinkingly at her until she began to feel uncomfortable.

Then she turned to King Toothbrush Weasel, and *didn't* throw her arms around him. In fact, she took a step back.

'OW,' said Malcolm the Cat.

'Oh, sorry,' said Ketch-up-Face, looking down and taking her foot off Malcolm the Cat's tail.

Then she looked up at King Toothbrush Weasel. He was dripping wet and **smelt** faintly of bananas, because as he had left the library a few minutes earlier, an enormous raindrop—about the size of a barrelful—had fallen on him.

'Well . . . bye, then,' she said.

'Come on,' said Stinkbomb. 'The bus'll be going in a minute!'

They both gave a little wave and made their way quickly over to the bus stop where the **Number 36 bus** was sitting, its engine **chugging** away merrily.

'Two children to Stupidity, please!' Stinkbomb said.

'Why, certainly, young gentleman!' said the driver cheerily. 'Welcome aboard! I'm Mr Jolly the bus driver! Can I check that it *is* the **Number 36** you want, and not the **36A**?'

'Er . . . what's the difference?' asked Stinkbomb.

'Well,' said Mr Jolly with a jovial wink, 'they both go to Stupidity, but the **Number 36A** takes the scenic route through the Valley of Despair, over the Mountains of Doom, across the Swamp of Misery, and past the Volcano of Death, while the **36**—that's this one—goes the direct route via the Traffic Lights of Waiting Rather a Long Time.'

'Oh, OK,' said Stinkbomb. 'Yes, it's definitely the **36** we want.'

'Righty-ho,' said Mr Jolly, a merry twinkle in his eye. 'Very wise, if you ask me. I probably shouldn't say this, but Mr Creepy who drives the **36A**, he's a bit . . . well . . . '

'Creepy?' suggested Ketchup-Face.

'Oh, no!' said Mr Jolly in surprise. 'No, I wouldn't say that. I was going to say "nervous". What made you think he'd be creepy?'

'Well,' said Ketchup-Face slowly, 'you're called Mr Jolly. . . '

'That I am!' agreed Mr Jolly happily.

' . . . and you *are* jolly.'

'That's true!' Mr Jolly exclaimed. 'That's a very good point indeed!'

'So I just thought,' Ketchup-Face continued, 'that if a bus driver called Mr Jolly *is* jolly, then maybe a bus driver called Mr Creepy would be creepy.'

Mr Jolly sat back in his seat and scratched his woolly, white beard. 'I never thought of that!' he said. 'Fancy me being so jolly when my name *is* Jolly! What a coincidence, eh? And now that I think about it,' he added confidentially, 'there *is* something creepy about Mr Creepy.' He scratched his beard some more. 'And he's not really nervous at all. I was mixing him up with the chap who drives the **Number 35A**. What's his name again? Oh, yes: Mr Nervous.' A look of delighted surprise came over his face. 'And come to think of it—he *is* nervous! Deary me!' And he burst into a **guffaw** of hearty laughter that shook the whole bus. 'Well,' he said, wiping the tears of merriment from his eyes and looking at his watch, 'better get going. It's nearly the end of the **chapter**. Take your seats, young lady and young gentleman.'

He was just putting the bus into gear when, from outside, there came a great shout of,

And they turned to see a crowd of raccoons racing across the square towards them.

# chapter 12

As the bus doors **hissed** open again, the raccoons swarmed aboard.

'Lots of raccoons to Stupidity, please,' said one of the raccoons.

'How many raccoons, exactly?' asked Mr Jolly.

The raccoons looked at one another, and shrugged. 'Dunno,' one of them said. 'We don't do maths. We're raccoons.'

Mr Jolly beamed. 'Well, young fellow-me-raccoon,' he said, 'how's about you give me 50p each, then? Be quick about it—we're running late! We should have left over a page ago.'

There was a lot of scuffling and mumbling about change, but finally the raccoons all had their tickets and took their seats, and the bus was on its way.

Everyone was very excited to be on the bus—especially Stinkbomb and Ketchup-Face, who had never been on a bus by themselves before because it was the sort of thing they were only allowed to do in stories.

It wasn't long, though, before Stinkbomb began to grow suspicious.

'You know,' he murmured to his sister, 'there's something odd about those raccoons.'

'Really?' whispered Ketchup-Face. 'Do you think maybe they're not raccoons at all?'

'It's possible,' Stinkbomb said.

'Shall we find out?'

'OK,' said Stinkbomb, 'but we'll have to be clever about it. We don't want them to know that we suspect anything.'

Ketchup-Face nodded wisely. 'Leave it to me,' she told him, and she turned round and said to the raccoon in the seat behind her, 'Excuse me, but are you *really* raccoons?'

The raccoon jumped guiltily. 'Oh, yes,' it said. 'We're definitely raccoons. We're very raccoony indeed. Never been raccoonier. Isn't that right, Rolf the Raccoon?'

'That's right,' agreed Rolf the Raccoon, a big raccoon with a big badge that said (Big Raccoon). 'We're raccoons all right. Aren't we, Harry the Raccoon?'

'Yes,' agreed Harry the Raccoon, taking a sip of tea from a mug marked, [World's Best Raccoon]. 'We're extremely raccoony. Aren't we, Stewart the Raccoon?'

Just as Stewart the Raccoon was opening his mouth to answer, Harry the Raccoon passed him a note that said,

Pretend we're raccoons.

Stewart the Raccoon read it slowly three times and then said, 'Er, we're raccoons.' He turned the note over. On the other side it said,

Don't let them know we're badgers.

'Er, we're not badgers,' he added.

'Oh, good,' said Ketchup-Face, reassured.

But Stinkbomb was still suspicious.

'Aren't
raccoons
supposed

# to have long, ringed tails?'

he asked.

'We *do* have long, ringed tails,' said Harry the Raccoon. 'Look!' And he opened a bag he was carrying and let Stinkbomb and Ketchup-Face look inside. It was full of long, ringed tails.

'Aren't those supposed to be on your bottoms?' asked Ketchup-Face curiously.

'Not when you're running for a bus,' said Harry the Raccoon. 'You might trip over them.'

Ketchup-Face nodded wisely; but Stinkbomb was still not satisfied. 'Are you *absolutely* sure you're raccoons?' he said.

'Absolutely,' said Harry the Raccoon. 'We've even got black masks on our faces.'

'Yes . . . but they seem to be held on with elastic,' said Stinkbomb thoughtfully.

'So?' said Harry the Raccoon rudely, but not too rudely because he didn't want anyone to realize he was really a bad guy.

Just then Ketchup-Face pointed out of the window, and said, 'What's that?'

Stinkbomb looked. 'It's the river,' he said. 'You know, the River Yuk. The big one that flows all the way from Stupidity to Loose Chippings.'

'What's it for?' Ketchup-Face asked.

'I don't think it's *for* anything,' Stinkbomb said.

'Though if it was cleaner I suppose you could swim in it, or fish in it.'

'And you could fill barrels from it,' suggested Stewart the Raccoon.

All the other raccoons glared at him and made **shushing** signs with their eyebrows.

'Er . . . if you wanted to,' Stewart the Raccoon added. 'But I don't want to. I don't like barrels. Or bins. I'm a raccoon.'

Then there was silence on the bus, as it trundled on towards Stupidity.

And then they reached the **Traffic Lights of Waiting Rather a Long Time**.

# chapter 13

In which we wait for rather a long time at the Traffic Lights of Waiting Rather a Long Time

'Right,' said Mr Jolly in a slightly less jolly voice. 'This is where we wait for rather a long time.'

And
they
did.

# chapter 14

In which we are still waiting at the Traffic Lights of Waiting Rather a Long Time

It got very boring.

# chapter 15

In which we are still waiting at the Traffic Lights of Waiting Rather a Long Time

**V**ery, very boring.

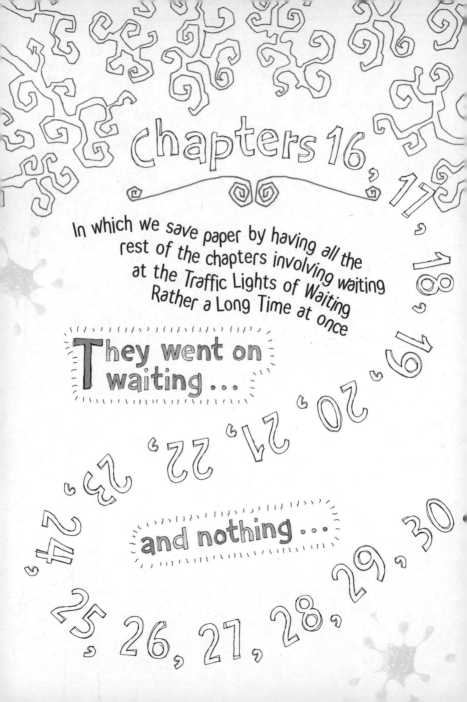

chapters 16, 17, 18, 19, 20, 21, 22, 23, 24, 25, 26, 27, 28, 29, 30

In which we save paper by having all the rest of the chapters involving waiting at the Traffic Lights of Waiting Rather a Long Time at once

They went on waiting . . .

and nothing . . .

31, 32, 33, 34, 35, 36, 37, 38, 39, 40, 41, 42, 43, 44, 45, 46 and 47

interesting...

happened.

# chapter 48

In which, quite unexpectedly, there is a bit more waiting at the Traffic Lights of Waiting Rather a Long Time

'Surely the lights should have changed by now!' Stinkbomb grumbled. He was beginning to wish they had gone the other way and crossed the Valley of Despair, climbed the Mountains of Doom, made their way across the Swamp of Misery, and faced the Volcano of Death instead. He was sure it would have been more interesting.

Ketchup-Face jumped up and pointed down the bus and out through the big window at the back.

'Look!' she cried. 'It's the mobile library.'

She waved at the nice lady who was driving the mobile library, and the nice lady waved back. It was Miss Tibbles, who ran Bouncy Sing & Clap Story Time for toddlers at the main library.

Ketchup-Face waved again, and so did Stinkbomb, and Miss Tibbles waved back again, and pulled a funny face. The raccoons joined in too. A few of them got very excited and began to be a bit silly, and some of them even showed Miss Tibbles their long, ringed tails and waggled them about, which sounds rude until you remember that their tails were in a bag and not on their bottoms.

And so they kept themselves amused while they waited for the lights to change.

# chapter 49

In which, at last, the lights change and the bus moves off

At last, the lights changed and the bus moved off. And Stinkbomb and Ketchup-Face and the raccoons went on waving and pulling faces at Miss Tibbles until the **rocking** of the bus made them sleepy, and one by one they all sat back in their seats and dozed off.

# Chapter 50

In which the bus finally reaches Stupidity

The bus juddered to a halt. From all around came the sound of raccoons yawning and stretching.

'Eeeek!' squeaked Stewart the Raccoon, as he opened his eyes.

'We're surrounded by bandits!'

Harry the Raccoon clipped him round the ear. 'That's not bandits,' he said gruffly. 'That's our reflections in the windows.'

'Lady and gentleman and raccoons, welcome to Stupidity!' said Mr Jolly.

The bus door opened with a **hiss**—and everyone froze in horror. There, right at the foot of the steps, was a deadly snake. It raised its hooded head, displaying its lethal fangs. Its little beadlike eyes glittered; its gaze swept over them all before fixing on Mr Jolly.

'Excuse me,' it said, 'but does this bus go to the Valley of Despair?'

'No,' said Mr Jolly cheerily, 'that's the **36A** you'll be wanting, young fellow-me-deadly-snake. It should be along in a bit.'

'Oh, thanks,' said the deadly snake happily. 'I was afraid I was going to be late for tea again.'

'I probably shouldn't say this,' Mr Jolly added, as the deadly snake **slithered** back a little to let Stinkbomb, Ketchup-Face, and the raccoons off the bus, 'but watch out for Mr Creepy, the driver. He's a bit . . . well . . . '

'Creepy?' suggested the deadly snake.

'Oh, no!' said Mr Jolly in surprise. 'No, I wouldn't say that at all. I was going to say "short-tempered".' He paused, and scratched his beard. 'Or maybe I'm getting him mixed up with the man who drives the **Number 33**. Now, what's his name again . . . ?'

'Right,' said Stinkbomb, as he and Ketchup-Face and the raccoons made their way across the little village square, 'where's this Magic Porcupine?'

Stupidity was a tiny little village. Aside from

the bus stop there was nothing in it except two houses stuck together, and a mud hut. There was no shop; there was no cinema; there was no post office; there was no pub; there wasn't even a nuclear research facility or a space shuttle launch-pad.

There was, however, a mobile library, which had just pulled up in the middle of the village square. As Miss Tibbles opened the doors, Stewart the Raccoon raced excitedly across to it.

'Excuse me,' he said. 'Can I have a 99, please?'

Miss Tibbles smiled. 'No, my lovely,' she said kindly. 'This isn't an ice cream van; it's a mobile library.'

'Oh,' said Stewart the Raccoon sadly.

'I know,' said Stinkbomb. 'Let's ask Miss Tibbles.'

'Hello, you two,' Miss Tibbles greeted them. 'Aren't your parents with you today?'

'Oh, no,' said Ketchup-Face. 'They like to stay out of the way when we're in a story.'

Miss Tibbles went a bit pink. 'Are we in a story?' she said. 'Oh, dear. Does my hair look all right?'

'It looks really nice,' Stinkbomb assured her. 'Do you know anything about the Magic Porcupine?'

'Oh, yes,' Miss Tibbles said. 'It's quite lovely, the Magic Porcupine is. And it's very, very magical. It can do the most amazing things. Why do you ask?'

'Well,' said Stinkbomb, 'the badgers have escaped from prison, and the only one who can foil their **evil** and **wicked** plans is the Magic Porcupine, so we're on a quest to find it.'

'And, er, we'd like to see it do some magic,' added Harry the Raccoon, who—along with all the other raccoons—had come over to join them.

Miss Tibbles nodded wisely. 'Well,' she said, 'you might try that mud hut over there. That's where it lives.'

'Oh,' said Ketchup-Face. 'Thanks.'

# chapter 51

In which our heroes meet
the Magic Porcupine of Stupidity

The mud hut was dark inside, and dimly lit by candles. Black shadows on the walls danced a strange and eerie dance, like your granny at Christmas when she's had too much fizzy wine.

Ketchup-Face edged closer to Stinkbomb and took his hand. 'It will be a *nice* Magic Porcupine, won't it?'

'Dunno,' said Stinkbomb. He was secretly hoping the Magic Porcupine would be like a grumpy old wizard with lightning flashing from his staff and a habit of saying 'Bah!' a lot.

Suddenly, the candles **flamed** and **flared** wildly, and a figure stepped from the shadows.

It was the Magic Porcupine of Stupidity.

'Oooooh,'

went all the raccoons excitedly.

It was hard to see the Magic Porcupine clearly in the dimness and gloom of the hut, but Stink-bomb and Ketchup-Face could make out the shape of the long, sharp quills that covered its body, and the **tall** wizardy hat on its head. The whole effect was jolly mysterious, and very exciting, and *extremely* magical.

'Um . . . hello, everybody,' said the Magic Porcupine. 'Would you like to see some magic?'

'Oooh, yes, please!'

said all the raccoons.

Stinkbomb hugged himself excitedly. 'Maybe it'll conjure lightning from the skies!' he whispered to his sister. 'Or make the whole hut fly up into the air! Or make a fountain of gold coins spring up from the earth!'

'Or turn a prince into a handsome frog!' Ketchup-Face suggested.

'Right, then,' said the Magic Porcupine. 'Pick a card—any card.'

'Um . . . this one!' said Harry the Raccoon.

'Look at it, and put it back in the pack,' said the Magic Porcupine. 'And . . . is *this* your card?' It plucked the ten of diamonds from the top of the pack and held it up triumphantly.

Harry the Raccoon shrugged. 'Can't remember,' he said. 'I think mine was that sort of colour, though.'

'It was definitely that shape,' added Stewart the Raccoon helpfully.

The Magic Porcupine sagged a little. 'Oh, well,' it said. 'Let's try something else, then. Erm . . .

Abracadabra!'

It reached forward and plucked a small coin from behind Ketchup-Face's ear.

# 'Oooh,'

said all the raccoons politely, and clapped.

But Stinkbomb was not so easily impressed. 'There's something funny about this,' he said. 'We need a better look at this Magic Porcupine. Where's the light switch?'

Ketchup-Face peered into the gloom. 'I don't think there is one,' she said.

'Oh,' said Stinkbomb. 'Well . . . hang on, I think I've got one in my pocket.'

Sure enough, a quick fumble in his pocket produced a square, white plastic light switch.

'Right,' he said. 'Ready?'

Ketchup-Face nodded. Stinkbomb pressed the switch.

The mud hut was

flooded

with

light.

The Magic Porcupine was magically producing a bunch of flowers out of thin air. But as the lights blazed on, everyone could see that it was actually whipping them out from underneath its **tall** wizardy hat.

'Oh, dear!' said the Magic Porcupine, trying to stuff the flowers back under its hat so quickly that the hat fell off, revealing a pair of **tall** floppity ears.

'You're not doing real magic at all!' said Stink-bomb.

'And I don't think you're even a proper porcupine!' added Ketchup-Face.

'I am!' said the Magic Porcupine unconvincingly.

'Then why have you got a zip up your front?' asked Stinkbomb.

'And why do you have such **tall** floppity ears?' added Ketchup-Face.

'Yeah!' said Stinkbomb. 'You're not a Magic Porcupine at all—you're just a rabbit in a **spiky** coat!'

The Magic Porcupine's face crumpled. It pulled a hanky from the sleeve of its **spiky** coat and blew its nose into it.

'You're right,' it admitted. 'I'm not the Magic Porcupine.'

'Why were you trying to trick us, you naughty rabbit?' demanded Ketchup-Face.

The rabbit burst into tears.

Ketchup-Face felt immediately sorry. 'Oh, please don't be sad,' she said.

'Yes,' said Stinkbomb, who was equally kind at heart. 'I'm sure you didn't mean to be naughty. You seem like a very nice rabbit.'

The rabbit sniffled again, and dried its eyes. 'I'm sorry,' it said. 'It's just that—well, this arrived this morning.'

It handed them a crumpled note:

Please may the Magic Porcupine be excused from being in the story today, as it has a bit of a cold and a sore throat, and I don't want it going out and making itself poorly before our holiday.

With every apology for the inconvenience,

The Magic Porcupine's Mum

'So you see,' said the rabbit, 'we needed another Magic Porcupine, or the story would just have stopped in the middle of **Chapter Fifty** without a proper ending or anything.'

'But why didn't they just get another Magic Porcupine?' said Stinkbomb.

The rabbit sighed. 'There aren't many really magical animals. And most of them already have jobs in those books about the boy who goes to wizarding school. So they asked me, because last week I borrowed a book about magic from Miss Tibbles. I've been practising really hard.'

'But you don't have any *real* magic?' asked Ketchup-Face.

'No,' agreed the rabbit sadly.

'But that means you won't be able to do any magic on the badgers,' said Stinkbomb. 'And that means you won't be able to defeat them and put an end to their **evil** and **wicked** doings.'

'And *that* means,' put in Harry the Raccoon, 'that we don't need our disguises!'

And with a **twang** of elastic, all the raccoons took off their black masks, revealing themselves to be none other than . . .

'Gosh,' said Stinkbomb. 'That was unexpected.'

'So Harry the Raccoon was really Harry the Badger all the time!' Ketchup-Face gasped. 'And Rolf the Raccoon was really Rolf the Badger, and Stewart the Raccoon was really Stewart the Badger!'

# 'Ah! Ah ha ha ha ha ha!'

chuckled Harry the Raccoon. 'That's what was so clever about our **evil** and **wicked** plan!' He straightened up and put on a big badge that said Big Badger. 'We fooled you completely! I am actually Rolf the Badger!'

'Yeah,' said Rolf the Raccoon, stepping down off the **tall** platform shoes that nobody had noticed he was wearing, and taking off the coat that was exactly like his own fur, only bulkier and with a big badge that said (Big Raccoon) pinned to it. 'And I'm really Harry the Badger. So there.'

Everybody looked at Stewart the Raccoon, who just shrugged and shuffled his paws and said in a small voice,

'Nobody wanted to swap with me . . .'

'Anyway,' said Harry the Badger, 'with the Magic Porcupine out of the way, nothing can stop us doing some **evil** and **wicked** doings!'

'*We* can!' said Stinkbomb bravely.

'Oh, yeah?' said Harry the Badger. 'Well, not if we tie you up and throw you in the river!'

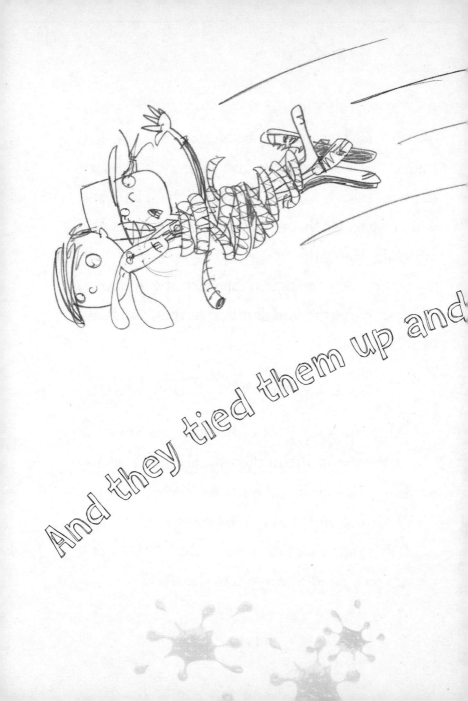

And they tied them up and

threw them in the river.

# chapter 53

In which the badgers make their getaway, and our heroes find themselves in terrible danger

'**Help!**'

shouted Ketchup-Face.

'**Glub!**' said the rabbit, getting a face full of dirty river water.

'Why aren't we sinking?' asked Stinkbomb, being a practical sort of child. 'I thought the badgers tied us up before they threw us in the river.'

'That's right,' agreed Harry the Badger from the steep bank above them. 'We tied you up with really strong rope, didn't we, Rolf the Badger?'

'Yes,' agreed Rolf the Badger. 'Well, sort of. But we didn't use proper knots. That'd be dangerous. We may be the bad guys, but we're not that bad.'

'I wish we weren't the bad guys at all,' said Stewart the Badger sadly. 'I'd like to be a good guy for a change.'

'I know!' said Harry the Badger. 'Let's catch the bus back to Loose Chippings and get rid of King Toothbrush Weasel! Then maybe in the next story, with all the good guys out of the way, *we'll* get to be the good guys!'

'Does it work like that?' asked Stewart the Badger cautiously.

Harry the Badger shrugged. 'Dunno,' he said. 'But it's worth a try. Look—here comes the bus now!'

Sure enough, a bus was just pulling in to the village square. Displayed on the front were the words

## Loose Chippings

written in big letters. Below that, in smaller letters, it said

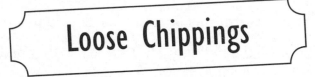

via the Volcano of Death, the Swamp of Misery, the Mountains of Doom, and the Valley of Despair

It was the **Number 36A**, and it was driven by a man who looked . . . well, a bit creepy, really.

'Quick!' said Harry the Badger.

The badgers all rushed across the square and scrambled on board, pushing past the deadly snake. Moments later, in a cloud of dust, the bus was gone.

'What do we do now?' asked Stinkbomb, treading water.

'Oh,' said Ketchup-Face breezily, 'something's bound to turn up.'

'Eeek!' said the rabbit.

'What do you mean, *Eeek!*?' Ketchup-Face demanded.

'Eeeeek!' explained the rabbit, pointing with a trembling paw.

Stinkbomb and Ketchup-Face turned, and froze with horror. There, cutting through the water towards them with terrifying speed, was a sinister grey triangular fin.

# 'Eeek!'

agreed Ketchup-Face.

# 'It's a shark!'

The shark began to circle them, drawing closer with each turn. Stinkbomb and Ketchup-Face, still treading water, clutched each other for comfort, letting out little whimpers of fear as the huge creature brushed their legs.

And then the shark spoke. Its voice came up from the water, a menacing **rumble** that chilled their blood.

# 'I am hungry!'

# chapter 54

In which you have to read the chapter to find out whether or not our heroes get eaten by a shark

'**Eeeek!**' said the rabbit again. 'We're going to get eaten!'

The shark circled menacingly, displaying a cruel mouth full of jagged triangular teeth. Wheeling away from them, it turned and made a sudden dash back.

'*I am hungry!*' it **rumbled** again, butting Stinkbomb's legs with its wide flat head. 'I don't suppose you've got any bananas?'

'*Bananas?*' squeaked the rabbit.

Ketchup-Face said nothing, but suddenly looked slightly smug.

Stinkbomb eyed the shark more carefully. 'You're a hammerhead shark, aren't you?' he said.

'Yeah!' said the shark in surprise, raising one eye out of the water to look at him. 'How'd you know that?'

'Well,' said Stinkbomb, 'your head's shaped like a hammer.'

The shark thought about this. 'Ohhhhh,' it said. 'Hammer . . . head. Head like a hammer. That makes sense. Funny I never realized before. So . . . *do* you have any bananas?'

'Um . . . I think I might, actually,' Stinkbomb said, fumbling in his pocket and producing a small bunch.

'Thanks,' said the shark. It neatly snipped off the ends of the bananas with its teeth and **sucked** the fruit out, leaving Stinkbomb holding the empty skins. 'Yum,' it said.

'I didn't think hammerhead sharks ate bananas,' said the rabbit. 'Not that I'm complaining,' it added quickly. 'Eat as many bananas as you like. I bet they're loads nicer than rabbits and children. I just didn't think you *did* eat bananas, that's all.'

'Me neither,' Stinkbomb agreed. 'I thought you were a bottom feeder.'

'Ewwww,' said the shark. 'That sounds disgusting.'

'I mean,' explained Stinkbomb quickly, 'I thought you ate things off the bottom of the sea.'

'Oh, yes,' agreed the shark. 'I do that, all right. That's how I found out about bananas. I was swimming along one day, when a sailor holding a bunch of bananas fell out of a boat and landed on the seabed. So I ate them. And very nice they were too. The bananas, that is. I don't eat sailors. I gave him a lift home instead.'

'Where does he live?' asked Ketchup-Face.

'Here, on Great Kerfuffle,' said the shark. 'Down the river, in Asillyname. Which is funny, 'cos he actually has a silly name. He's called Captain Bonkers.'

'That *is* a silly name,' agreed Ketchup-Face.

'I stayed in the river,' the shark went on, 'just swimming up and down, 'cos he's been bringing me bananas and they're so tasty. But I haven't seen him since Tuesday, and I've been getting a bit peckish.'

'What do you do with the skins?' Stinkbomb asked.

'Oh, I just drop them on the riverbed,' the shark said. 'I've been dropping them in a neat little pile under the bridge at Loose Chippings. This morning some badgers came along with a barrel and fished them out.'

'The badgers!'

said Stinkbomb, his suspicions instantly aroused and his clever brain starting to put things together. 'Did they fish out anything else?'

'Just some water and mud,' the shark said.

'Was it the sort of mud that would make water horrible, inky-splattery, thick, wet, and darkly splodgy?' asked Stinkbomb.

The shark shrugged, which is difficult for something with no shoulders. 'I suppose it would,' it said.

'And the banana skins would make it **smell** faintly of bananas!' said Ketchup-Face.

'Exactly!' said Stinkbomb. 'But that doesn't help us stop them. We'll never get back to Loose Chippings in time.'

'You might,' suggested the shark. 'If I give you a lift. Hop on!'

'Thanks!' said Stinkbomb, scrambling on to the shark's back.

'Yes, thanks!' said the rabbit, clambering up behind him.

'Giddy-up!'

said Ketchup-Face, climbing on in front.

# chapter 55

In which our heroes go on an exciting
shark-back ride in a brave attempt
to save the day

Travelling on shark-back was gloriously exciting. It was even faster than the little shopping trolley, and it didn't keep veering off to the left or leave a criss-cross pattern on your bottom. On they sped, leaving behind them a great trail of white, frothing, foaming water that **smelt** very, very faintly of bananas.

'What did you say your names were again?' asked the shark.

'Stinkbomb,' said Stinkbomb.

'Ketchup-Face,' said Ketchup-Face.

'The legendary Magic Porcupine of Stupidity,' said the rabbit.

'Really?' said the hammerhead shark. 'You look more like a rabbit in a **spiky** coat to me.'

The rabbit looked a little crestfallen. 'I'm just the stand-in,' it admitted.

'And what's your name?' asked Stinkbomb. He was already looking forward to telling his friends all about his death-defying ride on the back of a shark, and thought it would be even more exciting if he could tell them that the shark was called Killer, or Daggerteeth, or Terror of the Deep.

'Felicity,' said the shark.

'Oh,' said Stinkbomb. 'Is that short for anything?' he added hopefully. 'Like Felicity the Devourer of Thousands, or Felicity the Great Death-Machine of the Ocean?'

'Nope,' said the shark happily. 'Just Felicity. I did have an uncle once who was called Arthur the Devourer of **Hundreds** and **Thousands**, but that was because he liked those little colourful bobbly bits they sometimes put on ice cream. Any time you had an ice cream, Uncle Arthur would come along and devour the **hundreds** and **thousands** before you had a chance to.' Felicity sighed. 'Poor old Uncle Arthur. It was sad, what happened to him.'

'Oh,' said Stinkbomb. 'What did happen?'

The shark sighed again. 'All his teeth went rotten and fell out. Apparently those things are pure sugar. Now they call him Arthur the Devourer of **Soup** and **Soggy Cereal**. It's a bit of a rubbish name, really.'

'Yes, it is,' said Stinkbomb, thinking himself lucky he wasn't stuck with a silly name.

'Oh, dear,' said the rabbit, **sniffing** the air and looking at the sky. 'It's getting late. I hope we can stop the badgers before the end of the story.'

'We will,' said Ketchup-Face confidently. 'It's that kind of story.'

'Besides,' added Stinkbomb, 'Felicity's going faster than the **36A**, and that goes the long way round. We'll get to Loose Chippings in plenty of time to warn everybody.'

But what Stinkbomb had no way of knowing was that the **36A** was no longer going the long way round. It had come to a sign that said:

---

# Diversion →

The road via the Volcano of Death, the Swamp of Misery, the Mountains of Doom, and the Valley of Despair has been declared temporarily unsafe due to some slippery mud on the road surface.
Please take the alternative route.

---

Not only that, but Mr Creepy had made the mistake of stopping the bus and getting off to have a wee, and of course the badgers had immediately stolen it—the bus, that is, not the wee. Now they were driving it too fast towards the unsuspecting village of Loose Chippings.

And there was no one there to warn the villagers of the avalanche of badgery badness that was about to sweep down over them.

# chapter 56

## In which the badgers drive too fast

The animals that lived near the bank of the River Yuk **sniffed** the air, and looked at the sky, and glanced at each other worriedly.

'Can it be . . . ?' whispered an old mole.

'Surely not,' muttered a toad.

'Could we be mistaken?' asked a water rat; and they all **sniffed** the air and looked at the sky again.

'It's true, all right,' said a squirrel sadly. 'There really is a one-in-seventy-million chance of any of us being killed or injured by an asteroid during our lifetime.'

'We weren't talking about that,' said the water rat impatiently. 'Anyway, one-in-seventy-million means hardly any chance at all.'

'You've more chance of winning the lottery,' agreed a hedgehog.

'Or getting struck by lightning,' added a thrush.

'Really?' said the squirrel; and it rushed off to buy a lottery ticket and a pair of rubber boots.

The other animals shook their heads sadly, and sniffed the air and looked at the sky again.

'It's true,' said the old mole. 'Those **wicked** badgers have stolen Mr Creepy's bus and are driving it too fast towards Loose Chippings.'

'And here they come now!' said the water rat.

As the **Number 36A bus** roared past, brimful of badgers and trailing a huge filthy cloud of dust and fumes behind it, the creatures angrily

36A Loose Chippings
via the Volcano of Death, the Swamp of Misery, the Mountains of Doom, and the Valley of Despair

made their displeasure clear. The mole **booed**, the toad **hissed**, the water rat **shouted** a naughty word, the hedgehog performed a short but powerful piece of theatre, and the thrush got out a catapult and a bag of snails. A blackbird **blew a raspberry**, a raspbird **blacked a blueberry**, a bluebird **rasped a blackberry**, and in the river a shoal of sticklebacks quickly made some placards and organized a demonstration.

But all for nothing. The badgers drove on, their attention focused only on their **wicked** and **evil** plans, on driving too fast, and on trying to find a radio station that was playing music they all liked.

As the bus disappeared into the distance, the squirrel returned, **sniffing** the air and looking at the sky.

'All is not lost!' it said, carefully tucking its lottery ticket into one of its rubber boots. 'Two children and a Magic Porcupine are coming down the river on the back of a hammerhead shark to save the day!'

'Now you're just being silly,' grumbled the water rat.

But even as it spoke, a magnificent sight appeared upstream. Felicity was swimming faster than ever, her mighty tail driving her powerfully onwards. On her back rode three heroic figures, like warriors of old only smaller and, in the case of the one at the front, rather more ketchup-stained. It was so completely splendid and awe-inspiring that suddenly and out of nowhere an invisible orchestra began to play a majestic and stirring theme tune.

The animals began to cheer, and the sticklebacks quickly changed their placards to read 'Hooray!' instead of 'Boo!'

Stinkbomb waved proudly. Ketchup-Face stood up to take a bow, and fell off into the river with a big splash, so Felicity had to stop while she got back on again.

And then the water rat shouted, 'Wait a minute! That's not a Magic Porcupine! It's a rabbit in a **spiky** coat!'

'Humph,' grumped the other animals. And they all sloped off crossly, while the dramatic theme music ended in a **discordant clanging** as all the invisible musicians fell off their chairs.

'I may be just a rabbit in a **spiky** coat,' shouted the rabbit unhappily, standing up and shaking its paws at them, 'but I'm the only Magic Porcupine you've got!'

But the riverbank animals had gone.

'**Boo-hoo**,' sobbed the rabbit.

'Oh, don't cry, sweet little rabbit!' said Ketchup-Face earnestly, and she stood up and threw her arms around it. '**OW!**' she added, pricking her fingers on its spiky coat.

This made the rabbit cry even more. 'It's no use!' it said. 'This story needs a *proper* Magic Porcupine. The badgers are going to win, and we'll have to spend the rest of our lives sitting on a shark!'

Stinkbomb thought about this. The idea of spending the rest of his life sitting on a shark certainly sounded interesting, but on balance he wasn't sure if he fancied it. So he decided to cheer the rabbit up.

'This story *does* need a Magic Porcupine,' he said. 'And you're right—you're the only Magic Porcupine we've got! We need you!'

'But all I can do is silly conjuring tricks,' the rabbit said, pulling a large spotted hanky from behind Stinkbomb's ear and blowing its nose on it—the hanky, that is, not the ear. 'How can I possibly help defeat the badgers?'

'I think I know!' Stinkbomb said, 'I've just thought of a Clever Plan!'

'Tell us on the way,' suggested Felicity, **sniffing** the air and looking at the sky. 'The badgers are going to reach Loose Chippings ahead of us after all!'

'Wheee!'

shouted Ketchup-Face, as Felicity's tail thrashed the river once more, and they took off like a mighty fish-powered rocket.

'Giddy-up, fishy!'

Mr and Mrs Neck and their children Samuel and Philippa were out for a bicycle ride by the river when suddenly a hammerhead shark pulled up beside them and the little girl on its back asked, 'Excuse me, have you seen some badgers driving a bus too fast?'

'Yes, we have!' said Mrs Neck. 'Not very long ago, actually. We stopped to say "Good evening" to King Toothbrush Weasel . . . '

'And suddenly a bus full of badgers roared round the corner going much too fast,' added Mr Neck.

'Yes,' said Samuel, 'and they stopped, and tied King Toothbrush Weasel up and threw him in the bus and drove off too fast again.'

'You know,' said Philippa, 'I think there was something suspicious about that. Should we tell someone?'

'No need!' said Stinkbomb importantly. 'I am Stinkbomb, and this is Ketchup-Face, and we have gone on a quest to Stupidity and brought back a Magic Porcupine to sort out the badgers and rescue King Toothbrush Weasel!'

'That's not a Magic Porcupine,' said Samuel. 'It's a rabbit in a **spiky** coat.'

The rabbit folded its paws crossly.

'Did the badgers say where they were going?' Ketchup-Face asked.

'No,' said Mr Neck, 'they didn't.'

'Although, just before they drove off,' said Philippa, 'they changed the display on the front of the bus. Instead of saying

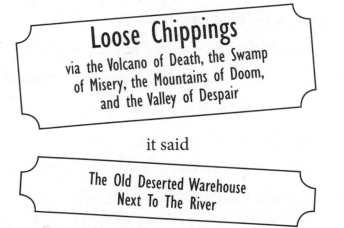

## Loose Chippings
via the Volcano of Death, the Swamp of Misery, the Mountains of Doom, and the Valley of Despair

it said

The Old Deserted Warehouse Next To The River

Does that help?'

'Yes!' said Stinkbomb. 'It does! Thanks!'

'Giddy-up, fishy!' added Ketchup-Face.

And with a mighty thrashing of a sharky tail, they were gone.

The Neck family watched them go.

'Do you know,' said Mr Neck, 'I wonder if perhaps those badgers have kidnapped King Toothbrush Weasel.'

'I was just thinking the same thing,' said Mrs Neck. 'I wonder where they've taken him?'

'Hmmm,' said Samuel. 'You know, if I were a bad guy, and I'd kidnapped someone and wanted to hide him, I'd probably take him somewhere not many people go. Like . . . '

'Like the old deserted warehouse next to the river?' suggested Philippa.

# chapter 59

*In which the story races towards an exciting climax*

The old deserted warehouse next to the river was very old, and completely deserted. It was also a warehouse. And it was next to the river, which meant that Felicity was able to take them almost to the door.

'Good luck,' she whispered.

'Thanks,' Stinkbomb and Ketchup-Face whispered back, and, along with the rabbit, they leapt onto the riverbank and crept past the abandoned **Number 36A** bus, and up to the entrance.

'Right,' whispered Stinkbomb. 'Here's the plan. We'll sneak in, and rescue King Toothbrush Weasel, and sneak out again. If we see any badgers, it's Clever Plan time. But we probably won't meet anybody, because it's an old deserted warehouse, so it's deserted.'

Quietly, he turned the handle and pushed the door.

All the people inside who were standing near the door moved out of the way to let them in.

'Hello!' said Mr Neck. 'After we talked to you, we thought we ought to tell some other people as well, and it turned out that everyone in the village wanted to come and help.'

'Then why aren't you helping?' asked Ketchup-Face.

'Oh . . . Well,' said Mrs Neck, 'it actually looks rather interesting, and everyone's decided to see what happens.'

It did look interesting. At the far end of the vast room, the badgers had built a stage, and across the stage was a large curtain.

'Well,' said Ketchup-Face, 'I don't care how interesting it is. If those badgers are doing it, it's probably an **evil** and **wicked** doing. 'Scuse us! Magic Porcupine coming through!'

'That's not a Magic Porcupine,' complained somebody. 'It's a rabbit in a **spiky** coat!'

The rabbit ignored him.

Just then, the badgers appeared onstage.

'Ladies and gentlemen!' announced Harry the Badger. 'Welcome to the end of the story! I know that most of you was probably expectin' an ending in which we all get caught and sent back to prison, but that'd be boring . . . '

'For us,' put in Rolf the Badger.

'Yeah,' agreed Harry the Badger. 'So we've thought

up a much more excitin' and interestin' ending.'

He pulled back the curtain, and everyone gasped; for there, tied to an enormous water rocket, was King Toothbrush Weasel.

'Blimey O'Reilly!' said Blimey O'Reilly.

'Gordon Bennett!' said Gordon Bennett.

'My goodness!' said Maya Goodness.

'Flippin' 'eck!' said Phillippa Neck.

'Oh, dear!' said a roe deer.

'How did that deer get in here?' asked an elephant; but everyone ignored it.

'Stinkbomb,' whispered Ketchup-Face, 'there's an elephant in the room.'

'Yes,' said Stinkbomb, 'but apparently you're not meant to talk about it. I'm not sure why.'

'As you can see,' continued Harry the Badger, 'we've made the biggest water rocket in the world, and we've tied King Toothbrush Weasel to it.

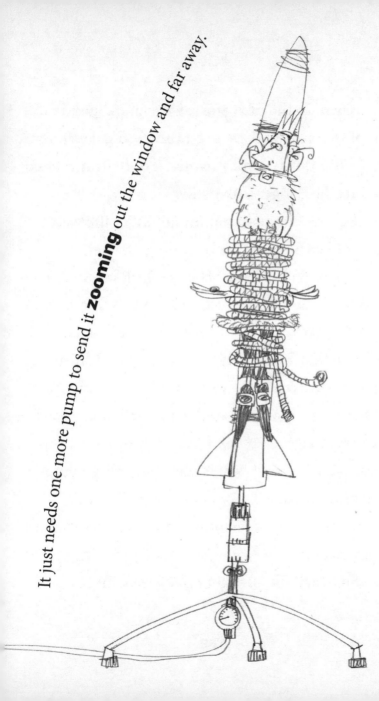

It just needs one more pump to send it **zooming** out the window and far away.

'Then, in the next story, with all the good guys out of the way, we'll get to be the good guys.'

'I still don't think it works like that,' muttered Stewart the Badger unhappily.

'But the good guys aren't all out of the way, are they?' asked Samuel Neck.

'Yes they are!' said Harry the Badger. 'We've defeated King Toothbrush Weasel by tying him to a giant water rocket; and we've defeated Stinkbomb and Ketchup-Face by tying them up and throwing them in the river; and we've defeated the librarians by messing up all the books in the library so it'll take them ages to put 'em all back in their proper places; and we've defeated the army by giving it a dish of cat food.'

'Yum,' agreed Malcolm the Cat from the front of the stage.

'So,' Harry the Badger cried, 'we win!'

# chapter 60

In which the exciting climax of the story actually happens

'No, you don't!' called Stinkbomb, as he, Ketchup-Face, and the rabbit pushed their way to the front.

'Grrr!' growled Harry the Badger. 'Yes, we do!' he added, as several of the badgers leapt forward and grabbed them.

'No you don't!' insisted Stinkbomb, as the badgers who had grabbed hold of the rabbit let go again, yelping with pain, and began sucking their paws. 'We have gone on a quest to Stupidity and brought back this Magic Porcupine to put an end to your **evil** plans!'

'But . . . that's not a Magic Porcupine!' said King Toothbrush Weasel from above them. 'It's a . . .'

'Yes, yes, all *right!*' said the rabbit in a fury, tearing off its **spiky** coat and flinging it down on the stage.

'Oh,' said King Toothbrush Weasel. 'It *is* a Magic Porcupine after all. I got confused because it was wearing a **spiky** coat that made it look like a dolphin.'

'Well, whatever it is,' **growled** Harry the Badger, 'it doesn't have any real magic, so it can't do anything to stop us.'

'Maybe I can't,' admitted the rabbit, 'but would you like to see some magic tricks anyway?'

# 'Oooh, yes, please!'

shouted the audience.

The badgers looked at each other and shrugged. 'Might as well,' said Rolf the Badger.

'Goody!' said Stewart the Badger.

'Right,' said the rabbit. 'For my first trick, I need some volunteers. **Evil** and **wicked** volunteers. Black-and-white ones, preferably.'

'Us!' said the badgers excitedly.

'Hmm,' said the rabbit. 'OK.' And it pulled a pack of cards from behind Rolf the Badger's ear.

# 'Oooooh!'

went everybody.

'Now,' the rabbit said to the badgers. 'Pick a card. Any card. But don't look at it.'

Each badger took a card and held it face down. Stinkbomb and Ketchup-Face held their breath, hoping the Clever Plan would work.

'Now,' said the rabbit, 'look at your cards.'

The badgers did so. Their faces fell.

'Awwwww!'

they said.

The rabbit looked suddenly very pleased with itself. 'Show everyone your cards,' it said.

'Do we *have* to?' whined the badgers.

'Yes,' the rabbit said. 'You volunteered.'

'All *right*,' sighed the badgers; and they held up the cards. As if by magic, each was now an identical peach-coloured card on which was printed a little picture of a barred window and the words:

GO TO JAIL.
GO DIRECTLY TO JAIL.
DO NOT PASS 'GO'.
Do not collect any worms
or dustbins.

'Do we *have* to?' the badgers asked again.

'Yes, you do, you naughty badgers!' said Ketchup-Face triumphantly; and Stinkbomb added, 'So there!'

'Come along,' said a cheerful voice from the crowd. It was Mr Jolly. 'I'll take you there right now, you little scamps.'

'Be careful they don't escape,' said Stinkbomb. 'It's just the sort of **evil** and **wicked** thing they *would* do.'

'No chance of that, young fellow-me-lad,' Mr Jolly assured him happily. 'I'll take a couple of the other bus drivers along with me to keep an eye on them. I reckons Mr Big and Mr Scary ought to keep them in order. And maybe Mr Useless.' Then he rubbed his chin. 'Actually,' he said confidentially, 'maybe I won't take Mr Useless. He's a bit . . . well . . . '

'Is anybody going to get me down from here?' King Toothbrush Weasel snapped.

'That cat food was nice,' said Malcolm the Cat, licking his whiskers and stepping backwards. `Ouch!' he added, landing on the **spiky** coat and leaping off again . . .

. . . only to land, to everyone's horror, on the pump. With a ***bang!*** and a tremendous ***whooosh!*** the gigantic water rocket shot towards the window

—with King Toothbrush Weasel still tied firmly to it.

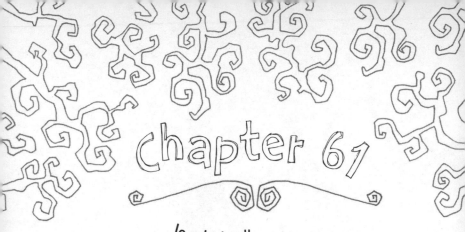

## chapter 61

### In which all ends well

'Eeeeek!' squealed King Toothbrush Weasel; and then everything happened in a blur.

In the instant before the water rocket struck the great window of the warehouse, the glass shattered from the *outside*. A **tall** figure dressed in black somersaulted gracefully through it. In a single elegant movement she drew her sword, cut through the ropes that held the king, and seized him in her arms. Turning in the air, she dropped silently to earth and landed, light as a feather, on the stage.

'OW,' said Malcolm the Cat.

'*Oh, sorry,*' said Miss Butterworth, looking down and taking her foot off Malcolm the Cat's tail.

'My hero!' said King Toothbrush Weasel, and fainted. Then he unfainted for a moment, just to say, 'Miss Butterworth, I mean; not Malcolm the Cat,' and fainted again.

And so everything ended happily; and as night drew in, joyous and peaceful sounds could be heard all over the tiny kingdom of Great Kerfuffle.

In Stupidity, there was the sound of a slightly **sniffly** Magic Porcupine being tucked in and having a bedtime story.

In the Loose Chippings Library, there was the sound of Miss Tibbles making all the badgers put the books back in their correct places before

Mr Jolly and his friends took them back to jail—
the badgers, that is, not the books.

In a hedgerow by the road that runs along the
River Yuk, there was the sound of animals watch-
ing TV together; a sudden '**Whoopee!**'; a burst of
joyful **scampering** through the undergrowth;
a happy cry of, 'I've won! I'm rich! I'm rich!';
a **crackle** of lightning; a **squeaky** `OW!`
and then a **thump** and a complaint of, `Ouch!`
My toe! Who left that asteroid there?'

And in Loose Chippings, outside the old
deserted warehouse next to the river, the famous
Magic Rabbit of Stupidity was giving conjuring
lessons to a hammerhead shark, a king, a well-fed
army, a Ninja Librarian, a little shopping trolley,
and a very contented Stinkbomb and Ketchup-
Face, who felt that only one more thing could make
the evening absolutely perfect.

Then a boat came **chugging** up the river, and Felicity joyfully cried, 'Captain Bonkers!'

'Ah-haar, me sharky!'

Captain Bonkers replied happily. 'Would you believe, the whole island ran out of bananas, so I sailed off to get you some more! And on me way back upstream, I picked up a couple of passengers . . .'

And Stinkbomb's and Ketchup-Face's hearts leapt as they saw two familiar shapes silhouetted in the porthole of the cabin door. And the door began to open.

'Mum! Dad!'

cried Stinkbomb.

'HELLO, MY DARLINGS!'

came their mother's voice from inside the cabin.

# 'CAN WE COME OUT? HAS THE STORY FINISHED YET?'

'Yes!' said Ketchup-Face happily.

# How to do a Magic Trick
## by Ketchup-Face

♦ First you need a volunteer. Parents are good for this sort of thing even if they do tut and sigh and say 'Oh all right then but be quick 'cos I have to send this email by five o'clock.'

♣ Get the volunteer to pick a card, show it to you, and put it back in the pack.

♥ Point behind them and say, 'Gosh! Look at that!' in a gosh-look-at-that kind of voice.

♠ Get your brother to do something really interesting just where you're pointing, like dancing in a funny way or juggling fruit or teaching a lion to ride a bicycle. If you haven't got a brother, a King or a librarian will do.

♦ While the volunteer is looking at the interesting something, look through the pack until you find their card.

♣ Stick the card behind their ear without them noticing. If they've got sticky-out ears, you might have to use sellotape or glue or chewing gum. (If you use chewing gum try not to get it stuck in their hair 'cos if they find out you'll get in trouble. If they don't find out, then next morning they'll probably have a pillow stuck to their head.)

♥ Tell your brother to stop doing the interesting thing, even if he's at the best bit.

♠ Pull the card from behind the volunteer's ear.

♦ Ta-daaaa!
It's their card. Magic!

It could be any card . . .
it doesn't have to be the
King of clubs!

K
♣

# Acknowledgements

Once more, thanks to all those children from whose games and foolery I've magpied bits of this book. Oh, and thanks to my friend Rob Kempner, who should have had a big 'thanks' in the acknowledgements of the last book for transcribing the music for 'Blueberry Jam' for me.

And 'hello' to everyone at West Earlham Junior School, where I'm very proud to be Patron of Reading!

# John Dougherty
## (Author)

*I still like to write about Stinkbomb and Ketchup-face!*

—if you want to know any more than this why not look here . . .
**www.visitingauthor.com**

# David Tazzyman
## (Illustrator)

*I still like to draw badgers!*

—if you want to know any more than this why not look here . . .
**www.davidtazzyman.com**

Look out for a brand new Stinkbomb & Ketchup-Face adventure in January 2015